Copyright © 2024 Michelle Burke
All rights reserved. No part of this book may be reproduced in any form without permission from the author or publisher, except as permitted by copyright law. To request permission, contact Author contact email
michelleburke@irishquill.com
edition number 1
Edition Published by Irish Quill

In a small, village in Donegal, there lived a little girl named Aoife. She loved to dance more than anything in the whole world.

Aoife would spend hours happily hopping and skipping, imagining herself on the big, bright stage. She loved the sound of her shoes tapping on the floor.

One day, she asked her dance teacher, Miss McGinley, if she was ready to dance at a Feis. But Miss McGinley shook her head gently.

Aoife felt a little disappointed, but she didn't give up. She practised every day, tapping and turning whenever she had a chance.

Every week Aoife asked Miss McGinley. "Am I ready for a Feis now?" But Miss McGinley shook her head.

Aoife practised more than ever before. She repeated her steps over and over, determined to dance her best.

One afternoon, Miss McGinley noticed something different in Aoife's dancing.

After Aoife finished, she asked one more time. "Am I ready for a Feis now?" Miss McGinley smiled.

"Yes, Aoife, you are ready!" Aoife's heart soared with happiness.

That night, Aoife laid her dress out carefully on her bed. She wanted everything to be perfect for the big day.

The next morning, Aoife and her family travelled to the Feis. The journey was filled with excitement and nerves.

When they arrived, Aoife was amazed by the sea of colourful dresses and the buzz of bustling excitement.

When she finished, there was a moment of silence before the room filled with applause. Aoife couldn't believe she had done it!

After all the dancers had performed, it was time for the awards. Aoife's heart raced as she waited to hear the results.

When Aoife's name was called, she was so happy! She had won a gold trophy. Mrs. McGinley had been right all along, now was the perfect time for Aoife to shine!

The End.

www.ingramcontent.com/pod-product-compliance
Lightning Source LLC
Chambersburg PA
CBHW042129040426
42450CB00002B/123